THE JUNIOR NOVELIZATION

randomhouse.com/kids

ISBN 978-0-7364-3047-0

Printed in the United States of America

10 9 8 7 6 5 4 3 2 1

THE JUNIOR NOVELIZATION

WITHDRAWN

Adapted by Irene Trimble

Random House New York

Up in a cold blue sky, two gleaming silver fighter jets thundered through the clouds. They leveled off and anxiously scanned the skies ahead. "What's taking this guy so long?" one of the jets asked, eager to face his competition. "Is he really as good as they say he is?"

"No," the other jet replied, and then smirked. "Better."

Like a bolt of lightning, a plane darted out of the clouds. There was no mistaking its sleek lines and smooth moves. They were legendary in the world of air racing. It was Dusty Crophopper!

"You ready to lose?" Dusty said to the two jets.

"Last one to the water tower buys a round of fuel," one of them replied.

Dusty chuckled. He was feeling generous. "Tell

you what. I'll give you guys a head start. You're going to need it."

"Later, loser," one of the jets said, and gunned it. The second jet was right behind him.

A confident Dusty watched them as he patiently counted off the seconds. "One one-thousand, two one-thousand . . ." Then he smiled and said, "That's enough." He instantly caught up to the jets and, in a sudden burst of speed, zipped by them both. "See ya, suckers!" he called back to the stunned pair. "Eat my dust!"

▰▰▰▰▰▰▰▰▰▰

"DUSTY!"

Dusty blinked and looked around. An old biplane named Leadbottom was calling to him. "Pay attention! You're daydreamin' again!"

"Me? No," said Dusty, a single-prop agricultural plane. He was momentarily confused. Then it all came rushing back. He was crop dusting an endless sea of corn in the middle of a field in Propwash Junction, Minnesota. There were no fighter jets in sight—only Leadbottom, his boss, flying below him. Dusty cringed when he saw that he had accidentally sprayed Leadbottom instead of the field!

He looked down at the rusty biplane and sighed. "Okay, yes. But c'mon. How hard is this? Fly straight, turn around, fly straight, turn around."

Leadbottom frowned. "Are you disrespecting the sweet science of aerial application?" he asked. Leadbottom had been crop dusting for decades, and he was proud of the trade that made the corn in Minnesota grow so high.

Dusty sighed. "Look, I am more than just a crop duster."

But Leadbottom was losing patience. "Don't go flap-jawin' about that Flings Around The Planet air-racin' nonsense again!" he grumbled.

"It's called the Wings Around The Globe Rally!" Dusty replied. "And it's not nonsense."

Dusty was convinced that he had what it took to compete with the best of them. "I've got a tight turn radius, a high power-to-weight ratio . . . ," he told Leadbottom.

"Oh, yeah, and ya know what else ya got?" his boss asked.

"What?" Dusty replied, hoping a compliment was coming his way.

"A screw loose!" Leadbottom declared. "I mean, why would ya want to give up crop dustin'? Blue skies, no air traffic, and that tangy scent of Vita-minamulch!" Old Leadbottom burped up a spray of the stuff. Dusty knew that no matter how long he dusted crops, he would never get used to that awful smell!

"Mmmm," Leadbottom said, savoring the pungent aftertaste. "Just like Momma used to spray."

"Ugh! Well, they say the sense of smell is the first thing to go," Dusty replied. Just then, he heard the sound of a train whistle in the distance. "Oh! Quittin' time!" he said as he zoomed off.

Leadbottom grumbled to himself. "Crop duster wantin' ta be a racer," he said. "Ya ask me, more racers should wanna be crop dusters."

But Dusty didn't hear a word. He was headed for town. As he reached Propwash's sleepy airport, he could see planes, tugs, and ground vehicles going about their business.

He flew toward the local gas station, the Fill 'n' Fly, where an old fuel truck named Chug was loading jerry cans onto a cart for a small tug named Sparky. Chug filled the cans and shook his head at the sorry state of the fuel business. "Nowadays they got soybean fuel, switchgrass fuel, algae fuel? Come on!"

"Ugh," Sparky said, shaking his head in disgust. "Healthy! No tank you."

"Tell me about it," Chug replied. "What's next? Pistachio propane? For my money, there's nothin' like good ol'-fashioned corn fuel. I even made up a slogan: 'Corn: It gives ya gas!'"

"Catchy! I like that!" Sparky replied with a grin.

Chug gave Sparky the last of the cans, and the tug headed off. "Catch you later!" he told Chug.

"Sure thing!" Chug replied. Just then, he saw Dusty zooming overhead. Chug's radio crackled to life. "This is Dusty Crophopper to Chug. Over."

Chug frowned. "Chug isn't here. Use the new call sign."

Dusty couldn't help grinning. "Oh, right," he said. "This is Strut Jetstream calling Turbo Coach Truckzilla. Ready for practice?"

"You betcha, Strut!" Chug exclaimed, and zipped off in high gear. He lived for the practice sessions with his best buddy. Chug knew Dusty had the heart of a champion, and he was proud to help the plane train for the Wings Around The Globe Rally.

As Chug headed for the cornfields, Dusty zoomed over a hangar and rattled its metal walls. An old World War II fighter plane named Skipper peeked out the hangar window.

He watched the young hotshot in the sky and muttered, "Punk."

Chug skidded to a stop at the edge of an airfield that overlooked miles of cornfields dotted with tall grain silos. He watched as Dusty flew out and circled back. "All right, buddy," Chug radioed, "I got ya in sight. Now let's start with some corn-row sprints! Drop and give me twenty!"

Dusty revved up the power and began his run as Chug consulted his trusty training manual.

"Nice turn!" said Chug when he looked up at Dusty. "Now let's try some tree-line moguls! All the way up and down. Don't be doggin' it!"

Dusty did a great job as he made his way up and over the treetops.

"Lookin' good," Chug said enthusiastically. Then he turned to another page in his manual. "Okay, uh, adjust your angle of bank with your alien-irons."

Dusty laughed at his friend's pronunciation of the word for the rudderlike control surfaces on his wings. "You mean *ailerons*?"

"Yeah, right," replied Chug.

Dusty was enjoying his run when suddenly his engine made a loud noise. He looked at his control panel and saw that the needle on his oil gauge was dropping. "Aw, great!" Dusty said to himself, knowing he must be leaking oil. He quickly radioed Chug, banked off, and headed over to see Dottie, the best plane mechanic in the county.

Soon Dusty was up on a scissor lift with Dottie peering under his hood. "Hmm, oil lines and oil cooler check out, AN8 fittings look fine," she said as she adjusted her headlamp for a better look. "Wait a minute." She narrowed her eyes accusingly. "You've worn out your main bearing seal."

"Really?" Dusty asked innocently.

Dottie frowned. "That kind of damage comes from extremely high speeds, pushing the engine to the red line for prolonged periods of time. But that's not you; you're a crop duster, and all you do is dust crops at very low speeds."

"Yep, low and slow," agreed Dusty.

Dottie looked at him suspiciously. "Unless you've been racing again!"

Just then, Chug came barreling into the garage. "Oh, man, Duster!" he said excitedly. "You were in the zone! Where a Saturn rocket couldn't catch ya! Ballistic! We're talking light speed! You're gonna tear it up at the qualifier this weekend." He saw Dottie's face and realized he had gotten Dusty into trouble.

Dottie stared at them both in disbelief. "*Dusty, you're not built to race.* You're built to dust crops. Do you know what will happen if you push it too far?"

Dusty and Chug felt a little guilty. Dottie had warned them that racing was dangerous for Dusty, and they hadn't listened. But that wasn't enough for Dottie. She began waving her arms. "Wing flutter, metal fatigue, turbine failure!" she cried. "'Oh no! I'm going down! Why didn't I listen to Dottie? She's the smartest mechanic in the world! Oh my gosh! The orphanage! Kids, fly out of the way!'"

Chug gasped in horror and cried, "Not the orphanage!"

Then Dottie made long, drawn-out explosion noises as she collapsed on her side.

Dusty was momentarily speechless. "Wow,"

he said finally, "that was vivid . . . and specific . . . and exactly why I need you to come with us to the qualifier!"

"You're unbelievable," Dottie replied.

Dusty grinned. "Ya hear that?" he said to Chug proudly. "I'm unbelievable!"

Chug looked over at Dusty with tears in his eyes. He was still upset over the imaginary orphans!

❊❊❊❊❊❊❊❊❊❊❊

That night, Chug and Dusty hung out watching RSN, the Racing Sports Network. They heard the announcer, Brent Mustangburger, say, "Be sure to tune in four weeks from now for the start of the Wings Around The Globe Rally!"

Dusty took a sip from the can of motor oil he was drinking and said, "Ya know, I think we've got a really good shot at this, buddy."

Chug held up his training manual and nodded. "Oh yeah, especially if I finish the book by then."

Brent continued, "And now, Racing Sports Network counts down *The Ten Best Air Crashes of All Time*!"

"Oh, I love this show!" Chug said excitedly.

He and Dusty winced as they watched planes skidding off runways and flying through billboards.

Chug looked nervously at his manual. "Ya know, uh, this might not cover *everything* you could run into out there."

"What are you getting at?" asked Dusty.

"I'm just wonderin' if maybe we need some help," Chug said.

Dusty seemed confused. "Help? From who?"

"Well, like . . . the Skipper?" Chug replied.

"That old Corsair down at the end of the runway?" Dusty asked.

Chug nodded. "Sure. He's a war hero!"

"He's an old crankshaft," Dusty replied grumpily.

But Chug knew that Skipper also had a lot of expert advice to offer. "My buddy Sparky says the Skipper was a legendary flight instructor in the navy. He knows stuff!"

Dusty wasn't enthusiastic. "He's been grounded for decades. Why would I wanna be coached by a plane who doesn't even fly?"

"At least he's a *plane*!" Chug exclaimed, reminding Dusty that he, Chug, was a fuel truck.

They turned their attention back to the television

as Brent announced, "And the number-one crash of all time . . ."

Dusty and Chug cringed as a huge collision lit up the screen. Luckily, no one was hurt. Still, the friends exchanged a worried look. Then Dusty glanced at Chug's training manual. For the first time, Dusty had the uneasy feeling that it wasn't going to be enough to keep him from becoming a highlight on *The Ten Best Air Crashes of All Time*! He turned to Chug and agreed that talking to Skipper wasn't such a bad idea after all.

Later that night, Chug and Dusty quietly rolled up to Skipper's old hangar. Everyone at the airfield knew that Skipper was one tough guy who didn't care much for visitors. A black piston-and-cross-wrenches flag flew ominously over the hangar door.

"They say he shot down fifty planes," Chug whispered. "I heard stories about his squadron, the Jolly Wrenches. They were the roughest, toughest, meanest fliers in the navy. Ruthless killers who showed no mercy. They'd shoot ya as soon as look at ya."

Dusty was getting nervous. "I hope you're right about this," he said as he pushed his wing against the doorbell. But Chug didn't reply. Dusty looked over and saw—no one! "Chug?" he called.

Chug peeked out from behind a barrel. "I'll

wait here," he whispered as the hangar door slowly rolled opened. Soon Dusty was staring into Skipper's scowling face alone.

"Ahhh . . . hey there, Skipper," Dusty said, trying to act calmer than he felt. "Say, uh, I'm trying out for the Wings Around The Globe Rally, and I know you can't fly anymore . . ."

Skipper shot him a menacing glare. Dusty realized he might have hit a nerve, and tried to recover. ". . . but, you know, they say 'Those who can't do, teach' . . . so, um . . . okay, what I mean to say is, you're not a truck, so I was wonderin' if you would . . . train me?"

The hangar door slammed shut. Dusty looked back at Chug, who was now even farther away. "Go on!" Chug called out from behind a building. "He's warming up to ya!"

Dusty nodded and rang the doorbell again. When the door rolled open, Skipper looked even angrier than before. Dusty thought he'd try a little flattery this time. "So, uh, I heard you shot down fifty planes," he said with a sheepish grin.

"You lookin' to be number fifty-one?" Skipper snapped back.

"No," Dusty replied quickly. "I figured with my guts and your glory—"

"Your guts would be a grease spot on a runway somewhere," Skipper said, cutting Dusty off. "Go home. You're in over your head, kid."

"Look, you flew all—" Dusty began, but Skipper slammed the hangar door shut again.

Dusty sighed. He couldn't help feeling disappointed and a little rejected. Chug wanted Dusty to try again, but Dusty knew that nothing he could say would change Skipper's mind. He headed back home.

CHAPTER 4

Dusty continued to practice without the help of a real trainer. Chug helped Dusty all he could, and Dottie stopped trying to talk him out of his plan, knowing it wouldn't do any good. Soon they were all on their way to Lincoln, Nebraska, for a qualifying race for the Wings Around The Globe Rally. Dusty was ready to give it his all!

As they approached the airstrip, they could see that the stands were packed with fans. The air was full of excitement as the racers and their service vehicles scurried through pit row, getting ready.

Dusty, Chug, and Dottie rolled down the tarmac. "I don't know how you talked me into coming to this," Dottie said to Dusty.

"Oh, come on, Dottie," Dusty said with a grin. He couldn't believe that anyone would be less than thrilled to be there. This was one of the most exciting racing events of the year! He and Chug couldn't stop looking at all the sleek racing aircraft around them.

"Check it out!" Chug gasped as a biplane did stunts overhead.

Two smaller racers named Ned and Zed took the microphone. "May we have your attention, please!" said Ned.

"Kindly direct your windscreens to the heavens above and give a warm welcome to our special guest," Zed instructed.

Just then, the sound of a powerful racer roared overhead.

"The Prince of Propellers!" Ned announced. "When he's speedin', he's leadin'!"

The plane he was talking about tipped toward the press and flashed a big smile. "Get my good side, fellas!" he told them.

"When he's grinnin', he's winnin'!" Ned added proudly. "The one and only . . ."

"Rip-SLING-a!" Ripslinger shouted as he tore through clouds of smoke. "You're caught in the RIP-tide!"

Dottie coughed as the smoke cleared. "With all

that self-promotion, at least he's modest."

"Dottie!" Dusty exclaimed, shocked by her sarcastic remark. "That's *Ripslinger!*"

"He's captain of Team RPX!" added Chug.

"They call him the Green Tornado!" Chug and Dusty said together.

"He's so good," Dusty went on breathlessly, "he's prequalified. Oh, and those other two, Ned and Zed, the Twin Turbos, they're world-class racers!"

Dottie still wasn't impressed. "You know, I hear they used to be one plane and were separated at birth."

"Wow," Chug said, "I wish I was separated at birth."

Dottie just shook her head. She couldn't believe some of the things Chug said sometimes!

The crowd cheered as the racers lined up. Dusty listened intently as the race official pitty explained the day's big event.

"Okay, people, this is the last of the four time trials being held worldwide," he said. "Today's qualifying round is one lap around the pylons. The top five finishers will qualify for the Wings Around The Globe Rally."

A racer named Fonzarelli rolled onto the runway. He would be the first to take the course. "He's through the start gate!" cried the official. "The racers must pass through the blue pylons on the horizontal and around the red pylons on the knife edge." Everyone watched as Fonzarelli navigated the course with ease. "Amazing pitch control—smooth, fast, clean. He's going into the final turn. Attacking the climb." The crowd stared in awe as the racer masterfully completed the loop and streaked to the finish.

"Now, that's some speed! A one-twenty-four-point-one-six," the official declared. "A very good time for the other racers to try and beat!"

Dusty was thrilled as he watched the next racer blast through the course. "He's got a great pace going here," the official said.

But just then, the crowd heard an engine sputter. They gasped as they watched the plane suddenly go down.

"Oh, engine failure!" the official cried. "Outta the race. Bye-bye!"

Another plane took off and tackled the course.

"Oh, no, he did not! That's a major penalty," the official said when the racer clipped a pylon. "Sorry, dude."

After several planes had completed their runs, a timer tug approached Dusty. "Okay, bud. You're up," he said.

It was finally Dusty's turn!

Dottie adjusted Dusty's wing as Chug filled his tank. "Fueled and ready, man," Chug said.

"Good 'n' tight," Dottie assured Dusty with a flourish of her wrench. Dusty took a deep breath and began taxiing toward the grandstands.

"Phew," he said to himself as he tried to gather his courage. "This is it."

As Dusty rolled down the runway, the race official was saying, "Well, it's been a wonderful day here in Lincoln, and we are down to our last competitor. Wow. From Propwash Junction: Strut Jetstream."

"Strut Jetstream?" Dottie asked Chug.

"Yeah. Awesomest call sign ever. It was my idea," he said proudly.

"We are looking for Strut Jetstream!" the official called again.

Dusty pulled up to the announcing stand.

"Hey, ag plane," the official said. "Get off the runway. We're racin' here!"

"I'm Strut Jetstream!" Dusty told him.

The official stared at Dusty and then started to laugh. "What's going on here? You're built for *seed*, not *speed*!"

Dusty rolled past Ripslinger, Ned, and Zed. Rip took one look at him and said loudly, "You gotta be kidding me. That farmer's gonna *race*?"

"Seriously? With a prop that small?" Zed added with a laugh.

Ned joined in. "Maybe he races that leaky ol' fuel truck next to him!" he teased.

Chug turned and shot back, "Who you callin' leaky? I'll leak on *you* if ya don't shut your intake!"

"Chug," Dottie said, "don't lower yourself to their level." Then she turned to Dusty. "Go on," she added encouragingly.

Dusty made his way to the starting line as the fans in the stands looked at him and began to laugh. He took a big gulp of air. He was trying not to let their sneering rattle him. But he couldn't help hearing them yell, "Who's that guy? Go back to the country! Cornfield's over thattaway!"

Dusty took his place at the end of the runway. It took all his self-control, but he blocked out the voices and focused on the task ahead. This was his one big chance—and he had to do his best.

"It's his first appearance at a time trial," said the official. "It's going to be a tall order for him to knock

Fonzarelli out of fifth place."

Dusty roared through the starting gate. "And he's off!" the official exclaimed as Dusty zoomed toward his first pylon. He was only ten feet off the ground!

"Wait! What?" the official shouted. "He is practically mowin' the lawn!" Dusty was flying low, but he was quickly picking up speed. The crowd watched in awe as he blasted through the course.

"Now he's only half a second behind Fonzarelli, and he is closing in rapidly," the official cried as Dusty headed into the loop. "He's back on that stick, up he goes . . . up and away! Now only two-tenths of a second behind."

"He's gonna do it! He's gonna do it!" Chug shouted as Dusty shot across the finish line.

"Oh, yes, what a finish!" the official said breathlessly. "Now, that's what you call flying!"

Dottie and Chug rushed over to Dusty, amazed. "Way to go, Dustmeister! That's what I'm talkin' about!" Chug cheered.

Finally, the official called the time. "Jetstream. Official time is one minute, twenty-four point two six seconds. Sixth place, but what a close one! Well, folks, that wraps up the tryouts for the Wings Around

The Globe Rally. It's been one heck of a day."

Dusty sighed as he looked at the leaderboard. He had missed qualifying by only one-tenth of a second!

Just then, Fonzarelli rolled up with a few kind words. "Hey, pal," he said. "Sixth place ain't nothin' to be ashamed of. That was a heck of a run."

Dusty smiled weakly and thanked him. But as the racer disappeared, so did Dusty's smile. He wondered if Skipper was right after all. Maybe he didn't have what it took to be a world-class racer.

Dusty returned to Propwash Junction and went back to his old routine—except it no longer included flying runs with Chug. He had packed up his dream of racing and tried to be content crop dusting the fields alongside Leadbottom. That was exactly what he was doing when a truck came barreling down the road, hitting every pothole roughly.

The truck skidded to a stop at Chug's filling station and backed up. A voice inside shouted, "Why don't you go back? I think you actually missed a pothole. You've got to be the worst, I mean the *worst* delivery truck that has ever delivered a delivery!" Then the door at the back rolled up, and a rattled-looking race official rolled out.

"Please tell me this is Propwash Junction," he said to Chug.

"Sure is," Chug answered.

"I'm lookin' for Strut Jetstream," the official said.

"Nope. Doesn't ring a bell," Chug replied.

"I have documentation that says Strut Jetstream lives in Propwash Junction," the official insisted.

"Oh, wait a minute," Chug said. The name *did* sound familiar.

Just then, Dusty rolled up. "I'm Strut Jetstream," he said. "But you're mispronouncing it slightly." He looked a little embarrassed. "It's actually pronounced Dusty Crophopper."

"Dusty Crophopper?" repeated the official.

Dusty scrambled for an explanation. "It's Scandinavian," he said finally.

The race official looked at the filthy—and stinky—crop duster in front of him. He made a face as he sniffed Dusty. "What *is* that?" he asked.

"It's Vita-minamulch," Dusty replied.

"Vita-minamuna-what?" asked the official.

Leadbottom couldn't resist chiming in. "The finest-smelling compost this side of the Mississippi!" he said proudly. "Original, creamy, and chunky style." He began to sing as he happily rolled away. *"I got some minamulch, yeah, I got some minamulch, yeah, some Vita-minamulch, early in the mornin'."*

The racing official shook his head. "That ol' airplane needs some help. Y'all know that, right?"

"Yeah," Dusty and Chug said in unison, nodding. They knew Leadbottom's enthusiasm for his job could seem a little weird to strangers.

Finally, the official turned to the business at hand. "Are you familiar with the racing fuel additive Nitro-Methane?" he asked them.

"Oh, yeah! Zip juice!" Chug said excitedly. "Go-go punch! That stuff'll blur your vision and slur your speech!"

"It's illegal," the official said, and then looked at Chug suspiciously.

Chug nodded quickly and began backpedaling as fast as he could. "Totally illegal," he said. "Wouldn't know what it looks like."

"That substance was found in the tank of the fifth-place qualifier," the official continued. "Illegal fuel intake is an automatic disqualification."

Dusty looked shocked. "Wait, so you're saying—"

"He's out. You're in," the official said flatly. "Congratulations."

Dusty couldn't quite believe what he was hearing, but Chug's huge grin convinced him. "You're in!" Chug shouted. Then the fuel truck turned to everyone else nearby and yelled, "You're never gonna believe this! He's in! Dusty's in the race!"

"What? Are you serious?" Dottie asked as everyone gathered around Dusty.

"Our Dusty, flyin' around the world!" someone shouted.

"I'd never try something as crazy as that," said someone else.

Chug was beside himself with pride. "Man, it's gonna be cool! You're gonna cross oceans thousands o' miles wide, freezin' your rudder off one day—"

"And burnin' it off the next!" Sparky exclaimed.

"Hurricanes, cyclones, typhoons, monsoons, tornadoes, sandstorms, gale-force winds . . . ," Sparky and Chug said, imagining the weather Dusty might come up against.

But as Dusty listened, his smile began to falter a little. This was going to be a bigger undertaking than he had thought.

After all the congratulations had ended, Dusty went back into his hut. He stared at the world map tacked to his wall and began to doubt himself.

"Bad idea," came a voice from behind him. Dusty turned to see Skipper in his doorway. The old plane had just heard the news that Dusty was going to be in the race. He looked at the crop-dusting plane and frowned. "You'll end up a smokin' hole on the side of a mountain with your parts spread over five countries."

"What makes you say that?" asked Dusty.

"You're going up against the best racers in the world," Skipper told him, "and some of them don't even finish. You're sloppy on your rolls, wide on your turns, and slow on your straightaways."

Dusty turned to Skipper with a glimmer of hope in his eyes. "You've been watching me?" he asked, surprised.

"Watchin' ya make a fool out of yourself," Skipper replied. "You need to be tighter gettin' in and outta your knife edge."

Dusty nodded eagerly. He knew Skipper was talking about when Dusty went from flying straight to tilting over and flying completely on his side.

"Any extra control input costs you speed and seconds," Skipper said.

"You think I'm overcorrecting?" Dusty asked.

Skipper nodded. "Absolutely. Rookie mistake."

"Are you giving me *pointers*?" replied Dusty.

Skipper was surprised. He'd thought all the mistakes he was pointing out would discourage the rookie. Now he could see that Dusty wasn't taking it that way at all. Skipper decided it was time to give it to him straight. "I'm tellin' ya to forget all this racin' malarkey!" he said angrily. "You just ain't built for it. You're a *crop duster*."

"You don't think I know that?" Dusty said angrily. "I'm the one who's been flyin' back and forth across the same fields day after day, month after month, for years. I've flown thousands of miles, and I've never been anywhere. Not like you. You were built to fight—and look what you did! You're a hero! I'm just tryin' to prove that maybe I can do more than what I was built for." He looked Skipper square in the eye. "You know what? Just forget it. You'll never understand."

Skipper sighed. He knew the kid wasn't going to give up. If Dusty insisted on racing, Skipper decided he had better help him. "Oh-five-hundred tomorrow. Don't be late!" he barked.

CHAPTER 8

The following morning as the sun rose over Propwash Junction, Chug, Sparky, and Skipper watched Dusty zoom over the cornfields. "Sparky, binoculars," Skipper said.

Chug admired the glasses as Sparky handed them to Skipper. "Those are some mighty clean optics there," Chug said. "What do you use, some kind of chamois?"

"No, it's a special microfiber cloth. Lint-free, scratch-free. I'll get ya some," Sparky replied.

"Really?" Chug said excitedly.

Sparky nodded. "I got an ex-navy buddy, sells 'em to me wholesale. I helped him set up his website."

"Knock it off!" Skipper finally barked at them. "We got a lotta work to do!"

Chug and Sparky piped down. Then Sparky whispered, "I'll hook ya up!"

"Thanks!" Chug whispered back.

"All right," Skipper radioed to Dusty. "Remember this: It ain't how fast ya fly, it's how ya fly fast. Show me what ya got!"

"Watch this!" said Dusty. He did some tree-line moguls.

"Great," said Skipper. "You can go up and down. What else? Show me your turns."

Dusty did some turns, but Skipper was not impressed. "You think that was good?" he asked. "That stunk. Knife-edge those elm trees! Keep your nose up!"

"Hey, Skip—" Dusty began, but his coach interrupted him.

"You want speed, right? Serious, bolt-rattlin' speed?"

"Oh, yeah!" Dusty shouted.

"Then look up," Skipper told him.

Dusty saw long parallel lines of stippled clouds that looked like streets above him.

"The Highway in the Sky," Skipper continued. "Tailwinds like nothin' you've ever flown!"

Dusty stopped smiling.

"What are you waiting for?" Skipper shouted as

Dusty maintained the same low altitude.

Dusty shut his eyes and pulled up, climbing higher and higher into the sky.

"C'mon, power up. Firewall thrust. Max torque! Looking good. Max rate now. Get your nose down. You're gonna stall. Ease off the pitch. Nose down," Skipper said, watching through his binoculars.

Dusty opened his eyes and looked down. Below him, the ground seemed to spin. Shaking, he peeled off and descended out of the clouds.

"Hey! What are you doing?" Skipper yelled.

Moments later, Dusty landed. He struggled to calm down and catch his breath as Skipper, Chug, and Sparky rolled up. "What just happened up there?" Skipper asked.

"I'm, ah, low on fuel," Dusty replied.

"Do I look like I was built yesterday?" Skipper asked angrily, knowing Dusty was holding something back. "The Jolly Wrenches have a motto: *Volo Pro Veritas*. It means 'I fly for truth.' Clearly you don't! Sparky, push me back to the hangar."

Dusty didn't want to lose Skipper as his coach. He took a deep breath and blurted out his secret. "I'm afraid of heights," he admitted.

"But you're a plane!" said Chug.

"I'm a crop duster. I've never flown over a thousand feet," an embarrassed Dusty replied.

"Scared of heights and you want to race around the world?" asked Skipper. He couldn't imagine what Dusty was thinking.

Sparky jumped in and tried to smooth things over. "Ah, Skip," he said, "during the attack of Tujunga Harbor, why, even P-38s had trouble at high altitudes."

"Well, they didn't have to fly over the Himalayas, did they?" replied Skipper, reminding Dusty of what he'd have to tackle in the race.

"I'll still be low to the ground. Just high up," Dusty argued.

Sparky nodded enthusiastically, hoping to win Skipper over. "After the war, those 38s went on to win races!"

"Really, is that true?" asked Chug.

"Oh, yeah!" replied Sparky. "Like in the Cleveland race of 'forty-six."

Sparky and Chug went back and forth trying to convince Skipper that Dusty's fear of heights didn't matter, until Skipper couldn't take it anymore. "All right! All right!" he said. "So you're a flat hatter. We'll work on that, but for now let's see if we can turn low and sloppy into low and fast."

"Roger that!" Dusty answered, grateful for a second chance. The two had an understanding. Dusty would tell Skipper the truth about everything from now on.

CHAPTER 9

At the next training session, Skipper had Dusty fly a slalom course through some silos. "The flag marks the start line," Skipper said. "Across the cornfields three silos are waiting for you. Slalom those with a radial G pass."

"A radial what pass?" Dusty asked.

But Skipper just kept talking. "Once you get to the trees, go to your optimal rate of climb, to about five hundred feet. Roll inverted and extend, trading altitude for airspeed, and dive toward the finish line."

"Okay," Dusty replied uncertainly.

"You string all that together, and you might have a chance to beat him," declared Skipper.

"Who am I racing?" asked Dusty. High above, a passenger plane was approaching.

"Here he comes," Skipper radioed to Dusty.

"He's a twin commuter pushing about fifteen hundred horsepower."

Dusty looked up nervously. "He's pretty high up," he radioed back.

"You're not racing him. You're racing his shadow," Skipper said. "Beat it to the water tower."

Dusty looked down and saw the plane's shadow as it passed over the ground. It was moving fast.

"Let's do this. Thread the silos. Tighter! Lean into your turns more!" Skipper urged. "Let's go, Dusty. Faster! You're falling behind!"

But the shadow passed the tower first, well ahead of Dusty. Skipper frowned. There was no doubt in his mind that if Dusty was going to have any hope of winning, he needed to improve his airspeed.

"So we can increase power or we can decrease drag," said Dottie. She showed Dusty a picture of himself—then ripped off the section with his sprayer.

Dusty looked uncomfortable. "Definitely increase power!" he quickly answered.

Dottie hooked him up to some machines to help him do just that, and then Skipper took over and taught him how to use the power. "Remember, now," Skipper said. "Altitude for airspeed. Gravity is your ally. The laws of physics govern speed."

Dusty practiced what he'd learned over and over again. One day, he managed to weave perfectly through the silos while still keeping an eye on the plane's shadow just ahead of him.

"That's what I'm talking about!" said Skipper excitedly. "Firewall the throttle. Go! Go! Go!"

Dusty picked up speed and climbed higher.

"Catch him in the dive!" cried Skipper. "Dive now!"

Suddenly, everything Skipper had taught Dusty came together. He closed in on the shadow and beat it to the tower!

Chug and Sparky whooped with joy, but Skipper just grinned. "He's ready," he said.

Later that day, as the sun set over the cornfields, Sparky spray-painted the Jolly Wrenches' logo on Dusty.

"Whoa," Dusty said to Skipper. "Your squadron insignia!"

Skipper smiled and said, "You've earned it. Now listen. When the race starts and all those planes take off, it'll stir up a bunch of swirling air, just like the Wrenches ran into in the Battle of Airway."

"Roger that," Dusty said. "Sure wish you were comin' with me, Skip."

"Just radio back when you get to the checkpoints. I'll be your wingman from here," Skipper told him.

"*Volo Pro Veritas*—right?" Dusty said.

"*Volo Pro Veritas*," replied Skipper.

Dusty beamed with happiness. His dream of flying in the Wings Around The Globe Rally was about to come true!

CHAPTER 10

The next day, Dusty took off for New York, where the first leg of the rally would begin. By evening, he was approaching John F. Kennedy International Airport. Dusty gasped when he saw the lights of the city twinkling below him. He had never seen anything so dazzling!

Just then, an air-traffic controller from the airport radioed him. "Break, break, Air Racer Number Seven, Air Racer Number Seven, do you read Kennedy approach, over?"

"Uh," Dusty mumbled, "I'm Dusty Crophopper! Lookin' for JFK Airport."

"Crophopper Seven, you are supposed to be on the Canarsie visual. Turn further left, heading one-nine-five. Maintain one thousand feet, intercept the twenty-two right localizer. You are cleared for the

ILS twenty-two right approach. Heavy sectored in behind you," the air-traffic controller said.

"Roger. Um, run that by me one more time," replied Dusty. All the technical language was confusing him. Then he saw the bright runway lights. "Never mind! I got it!"

The air-traffic controller tugs looked up from their radar screens to watch Dusty land. "Do you see him?" one asked, expecting to see Dusty land where he had been given clearance.

"Radar does, but I don't see diddly," the other controller replied. Then he noticed the little plane on a huge runway.

"Check out this pavement," Dusty said, impressed. "It's so smooth!"

Dusty's radio blared, "Crophopper Seven, you've passed Foxtrot. Turn left onto Charlie, hold short at twenty-two—"

"Huh?" Dusty replied. "Wait, I thought Fox . . . Isn't that—"

"GET OFF THE RUNWAY!" the controller yelled. A giant jet thundered over Dusty, just missing him.

Dusty zipped onto the congested tarmac and

dodged passenger jets and tugs. Horns honked all around him. "Sorry!" Dusty apologized.

"Go back to Jersey, ya bum!" somebody yelled at him.

Rattled and confused, Dusty approached another service vehicle that was loaded with luggage. "Excuse me, where can I—"

"Hey," the service tug said, cutting Dusty off, "you mind? I'm workin' here."

"Sorry," Dusty said again. Flight attendant pitties rolled by, pulling their suitcase-like trailers behind them. "Excuse me," Dusty said to one of them. But she didn't pay any attention to him.

Dusty heard her say, "Yeah, nice-enough guy, but way too much baggage, if you know what I mean." Her fellow flight attendants nodded sympathetically as they continued past.

Dusty, still lost and confused, nearly ran into a tug towing a huge 747. "Hey there," Dusty called out. "I'm looking for pit row."

The little towing tug strained as he answered, "Straight ahead and to your left."

"Thanks," Dusty said, finally feeling like he could find his way through the huge maze of the airport.

Soon he saw a banner near a row of tents and hangars. It read WELCOME, RACERS. Dusty was so relieved. He was finally in the right place! Many of the racers were already gathered on pit row along with their mechanic tugs. He couldn't wait to meet them all.

"Well, lookie who's here!" the race official said to Dusty as he rolled into the racers' area. It was the same official who had gone out to Propwash Junction to tell Dusty he'd be racing. "Miss your hometown?" he asked, and laughed. "I don't. Just about blocked that memory out of my mind, but you're bringing it right back with that nasty Vita-mina-stink-a-bunch." He sniffed the air around Dusty. "Your tent's the last one on the left. Go."

As Dusty rolled away, the official called after him, "Power wash is on the right. Just sayin'." But Dusty didn't take offense. This was the big time, and he was just happy to be part of it all!

CHAPTER 11

Dusty rolled down pit row, completely awestruck. It was even more colorful and exciting than the county fair in Propwash Junction. All the great racers from around the world were there!

He was thrilled when he spotted the British racer Bulldog. Dusty was a huge fan. He rolled up to the racing legend. "Wow, Bulldog! The Big Dog! Hey, I saw you do this unbelievable high-G vertical turn. How did you do that?"

"Well, let me tell you," Bulldog said, leaning in as if he was going to whisper something. "In fact, why don't I tell you all my racing secrets?"

"Really?" Dusty replied. He couldn't believe it—a superstar like Bulldog was going to give him flying tips!

"No!" Bulldog snapped. "Look, I don't know

how things work in the backwater from which you hail, matey, but this is a competition. Every plane for himself. Goodbye."

Dusty was shocked and a little insulted by Bulldog's unfriendliness. He turned to go and nearly ran into a beautiful, exotic-looking racer. He became so flustered that he knocked over a pyramid of motor oil cans. Dusty quickly tried to recover from his blunder. "Well, I am sorry you had to see that," he said nervously.

"Are you all right?" she asked.

"Sure, why wouldn't I be?" Dusty replied. "And *you* are Pan-Asian Champion and Mumbai Cup record-holder Ishani."

She smiled. "Most people call me just Ishani."

Dusty took one look at her smile and melted inside. "I'm Dusty," he said. "I mean, my name is Dusty. I'm not actually dusty. I'm . . . quite clean."

"It is very nice to meet you, quite-clean Dusty," Ishani told him.

Dusty watched her roll away. "Nice to meet you, too!" he called after her.

Dusty noticed Ripslinger's expensive setup. It was equipped with a DJ and an extravagantly lit stage.

Rip's crew was scurrying around while Rip enjoyed a relaxing massage.

He looked over as Dusty approached him. "Hey, look who made it—it's the crop duster!" Rip said with a laugh. "You know, having you here is a nice vehicle-interest story. 'Small-town farmer makes it to the big time.'"

"Yes, sir," Dusty exclaimed, liking the sound of it. He could imagine photos of him and Rip together at the starting line while millions of fans cheered them on.

Then Rip added, "'But tragically, he crashes on takeoff.'"

"What?" Dusty said, confused.

Rip gave him a big grin, enjoying his fantasy. "'Wings Around The Globe winner, Ripslinger, eulogizes the unknown hayseed and scatters his debris over a cornfield.'" Rip's smile seemed even more serene. "Ratings will be through the roof!"

Dusty was completely stunned. "Okay . . . ?" he said uncertainly as he turned to go.

"Good luck . . . farm boy," Rip said, laughing. Dusty realized that Rip didn't see him as much of a contender in the race. In fact, he barely saw him making it off the starting line.

But Dusty didn't think much more about it. His attention was drawn away by someone announcing, *"¡Atención, señoritas y señores!* The hero of the people has arrived!" Dusty turned to see a teardrop-shaped Gee Bee in a cape and a mask roar up. It was El Chupacabra. The masked plane waited for his applause, but no one cheered.

"Have you never heard of the great El Chupacabra?" El Chu asked the crowd.

One of the racers asked another, "Isn't that the monster that siphons fuel from small vehicles?"

"No, no, no," the masked plane said. "It is just a stage name designed to strike fear into the hearts of my opponents."

"Yeah," Dusty said excitedly. "He's the indoor racing champion of all Mexico!"

"Indoor racing?" Bulldog asked, a bit confused.

"And *número uno* recording artist, *telenovela* star, and romance novelist," El Chu added.

Everyone but Dusty looked at the masked plane skeptically. Finally, Bulldog said, "Did you say El Chupacabra or El Cuckoocabra?"

The other racers chuckled as El Chu fumed. He

stormed up to Bulldog. "You make joke?" he asked. "Very well. You leave me no choice! I swish my cape at you! You have been shamed."

"I hope I can get over it," Bulldog said. He waited a second and sarcastically added, "Oh, I just did."

El Chupacabra turned and haughtily rolled down pit row. Only Dusty followed him. "I saw you on Telemoto last year. Course, it was in Spanish, so I didn't understand everything."

"I am very flattered, *avión pequeño*! You have done many of these long-distance rallies, yes?"

"Nope," Dusty said. "This is my first one."

El Chupacabra nodded. "It is my first time as well. We will have many adventures, you and I! We will laugh, we will cry, we will dance! Probably not with each other." Then, with a flourish of his cape, he said, "I will see you in the skies, amigo!"

As Dusty watched him go, he was happy to have finally made a friend!

The following morning, the gang in Propwash Junction gathered around the TV set they'd set up in the main hangar. They watched with excitement as the Racing Sports Network graphic appeared on the screen. The announcer said, "Race fans, it's that time of year again! Welcome to the Wings Around The Globe! Hello, I'm Brent Mustangburger, and this is *the* flagship event of the world's fastest sport, where only the best of the best compete."

The graphics returned to the screen, showing the race's route around the world. "Each leg brings a new challenge, testing agility, navigation, and endurance. But when it's all said and done, speed is the name of the game," Brent said.

The camera jumped to a live shot of JFK Airport with Colin Cowling, the Racing Sports Network blimp, flying above it.

"Brent," Colin said, "the scene below me is absolutely electric. As you know, we have racers from all over the world here, but the real story should be who's coming in second to three-time defending champ, Ripslinger, who is seeking to become the first four-time winner in the Wings Around The Globe."

Now the cameras panned to where the racers were approaching the runway. Dusty's friends back home went wild. "It's Dusty!" cried Dottie and Sparky.

"Get your Dusty bobbleheads, your oven mitts, hats, bumper stickers . . . ," Chug said as he unveiled all his Dusty Crophopper merchandise.

"Coolio," Sparky said.

"I also ordered a thousand commemorative whistles," Chug told him. "Hey, ya think you could help me set up a website?"

"Does a giga bite?" asked Sparky.

"Well, not if you pet him nicely!" said Chug.

✖✖✖✖✖✖✖✖✖✖

Back at the airport, cameras flashed as the racers made their way through the entrance tunnel.

"One hundred and thirty-six nations compete,"

Brent Mustangburger said. "Twenty-one planes selected. A step onto this field is a step into history."

The crowd roared, and confetti rained down from the sky. "Holy smokes," Dusty said. It was all a bit overwhelming.

Then Brent said, "And for the first time ever, folks, we have a crop duster in the race."

The news was heard around the world. In a pub in England, a pitty looked shocked. "A crop duster?" he asked incredulously.

"Well, he's gonna die," another commented with certainty.

Meanwhile, out at JFK, three jets flying in formation roared over the heads of the crowd.

"Wow," Dusty said in awe.

Then Ripslinger taxied out and the crowd went wild, shouting, "Ripslinger! Ripslinger!"

"Yeah!" Rip said. "Caught in the RIP-tide!"

El Chupacabra came out next. *"¡Muchas gracias!"* he shouted to the spectators.

Dusty rolled up to him. "Look at this crowd!" he said excitedly.

"Stay focused, amigo. Don't let anything distract you—*¡Ay, ay!*" El Chupacabra said as his eyes strayed to one of the lady planes in the race. "Who is that vision?"

"That's Rochelle," Dusty told him, "the Canadian rally champ."

El Chupacabra was completely smitten. "She is like an angel sent from heaven. Like a sunrise after a lifetime of darkness!"

Dusty nodded. "Like fresh fertilizer on a field of dying grass."

El Chupacabra rolled his eyes at Dusty's unromantic comparison. "This is not your thing, my friend."

"Racers!" shouted the judge. "Start your engines!"

CHAPTER 13

The gang in Propwash Junction held their breath. Their eyes were glued to the television as Dusty revved his engine and prepared to take off.

"Seven legs over thirty-one thousand kilometers," Brent Mustangburger told his viewers. "The world's highest mountains and the deepest oceans all stand before them, just waiting to be conquered by the right competitor."

"Here we go! Oh, boy," Chug said, staring wide-eyed at the screen.

"All the predictions, all the pageantry, all the preparation . . . it all comes down to this moment," Brent continued. "One of these planes is about to fly off into the pages of sports history and become a champion."

While the racers idled at the starting line, they furtively looked from side to side, sizing each other up. Dusty let out a nervous breath as an official dropped a flag and the judge shouted, "Go!"

The planes began their takeoff and Dusty felt his wheels leave the ground.

"Whoa! Swirlies! Whoa! Whoa!" he cried as he bounced around in the turbulence made by the planes ahead of him. This was exactly what Skipper had warned him about! He dropped down and flew close to the water to avoid the choppy air.

The other racers soon spread out and soared over the waters of the Long Island Sound. Dusty stayed low and followed the coast, trailing behind them.

"Our first stage is a whopper," Brent said. "A dead sprint across the North Atlantic." The racers were flying all the way to Reykjavík, Iceland!

"That's right, Brent," Colin said. "This is how it works, folks. The winner of the leg today is the first to take off tomorrow."

When they reached Newfoundland, Dusty knew he had to give up clinging to the coast and fly across the vast Atlantic. By now all the other racers had climbed above the clouds—but Dusty was so low, he could see the whitecaps on the water!

It wasn't long before his teeth were chattering in the freezing cold. Hail began to pummel his wings and body, and snow swirled around him. He could barely see. A huge shape rose out of the mist to greet him. An iceberg! Dusty dodged it at the very last second.

CHAPTER 14

As the rest of the racers warmed themselves by roaring fire pits at the airport in Reykjavík, Dusty rolled in, shivering. He was the last plane to arrive.

"Hey, look who's finally here!" said Zed. "It's the low-flying farm boy!"

"You do know this is a *race*, right?" Rip asked.

Dusty faked a grin and kept going. He passed El Chupacabra but didn't stop to chat. El Chu was obviously busy trying to get Rochelle's attention.

"Excuse me," he said to Rochelle. "How much does a snowplow weigh?"

"I do not know," she replied.

"Enough to break the ice," he said smoothly. "I am El Chupacabra."

Rochelle smiled and nodded. "So you are the snowplow?"

El Chupacabra lit up. The beautiful jet had finally

noticed him. "You could say that, yes."

"And I am the ice?" she asked him.

El Chu smiled. "Yes?"

"Cold, frozen, and lifeless?" she asked.

"No. It sounds better in Spanish," he said, stumbling.

"Why don't you go plow yourself, El Chu-Toy!" she said as she rolled away.

El Chupacabra melted nonetheless. "She is like an angel!" he cried, undaunted by her rejection.

Cold, miserable, and exhausted, Dusty slumped into a corner. Just then, the nearby radio came to life and a friendly voice said, "Propwash Junction to Dusty Crophopper." Chug, Skipper, Dottie, and Sparky were calling!

"I read you, Chug," replied Dusty.

"So what's it like racing with the big dogs, Duster?" Chug asked.

"My wings froze solid, I had icicles hangin' off my sprayer, and I nearly smashed into a ten-story iceberg," said a frustrated Dusty. He still couldn't believe how much harder the race was than he had imagined.

But it was all lost on Chug. "Awwwesome!" he

replied, eager to hear more. He thought it all sounded kind of exciting.

"*Awesome* is not quite the word that I would use to describe a gruesome near-death experience," Dusty shot back.

"You hang in there, buddy," Chug said cheerily. "There's nothin' better than dying while doin' what you love most."

"*That's* gonna make him feel a lot better!" Dottie scolded.

Then Skipper got on the radio. "Dusty," he said. "Just like when the Jolly Wrenches were up in the Aleutians, the air down close to the sea has more moisture, which is why you took on ice. *You gotta try to fly higher.*"

Dusty exhaled. He knew Skipper was right, but he was completely unnerved by the prospect.

"The good news," Skipper continued, "is tomorrow's leg goes through the Bavarian obstacle course. It's all about agility, so it's your chance to move up. And remember: It's not speed that wins races; it's skill."

Dusty nodded and signed off. But he couldn't help worrying.

Dusty Crophopper was a crop-dusting plane, but he dreamed about being a champion racing plane.

Dusty got the chance to fly in the Wings Around The Globe Rally. He was excited—and a little nervous!

Skipper agreed to coach Dusty. He was surprised
to find out that Dusty was afraid of heights!

The Wings Around The Globe Rally started in New York.
Dusty met many of his racing idols, including Bulldog.

Ishani was also competing in the rally. She was one of the first planes who was nice to Dusty.

Dusty made instant friends with El Chupacabra. El Chu was flashy and fun to be around!

Ripslinger had won the rally three times before.
He was a show-off, and not very nice.

On the leg to Iceland, Dusty flew low and got caught
in a storm. Skipper told him to try flying higher.

Franz, a little car who could turn into a plane, told Dusty he'd fly faster without his crop-dusting gear.

Dusty moved up to eighth place—and became an overnight sensation! Ripslinger was not happy.

In the Himalayas, Dusty followed railroad tracks through
the mountains—and almost crashed into a train!

By the time the racers reached Shanghai, China, Dusty
was in first place! "I'm proud of you," Skipper told him.

When Zed broke off Dusty's antenna, Dusty got lost and almost ran out of fuel. Two navy jets rescued him.

Dusty got a new antenna and a tank of fuel before setting off for Mexico in a storm.

After Dusty had a bad crash in the sea, Dottie told him that he was too damaged to finish the race.

El Chu did not want to compete without Dusty. He gave his friend a pair of wings to replace his broken ones.

The next night, the racers headed off on the second leg of the race, which would take them from Iceland to Germany. Dusty was finally in his comfort zone. He flew low, and just like he had practiced weaving between silos in the cornfields back home, Dusty easily dodged the pylons and caught up to Bulldog.

Bulldog could see Dusty coming up from behind. He was increasing his speed and altitude to get away from the annoying crop duster when his cowling—the metal cover over his engine—suddenly burst. Oil squirted out over his canopy, completely blinding him. "Ahhh!" Bulldog yelled as he flipped over and started falling from the sky. "Mayday, mayday, mayday!" he radioed. "I'm blinded!"

A special graphic flashed across TV screens around the world. "We're receiving breaking news of an incident in the skies over Germany involving one of the racers," announced Brent Mustangburger. "Let's check in with Sky Cam One for more information."

Sky Cam One reported back quickly. "Bulldog, the legendary flier from the U.K., is in tremendous danger. It looks like he's flying blind, losing speed, losing altitude."

As Bulldog arced down, he radioed again. "Mayday, mayday, mayday! I need assistance. Is anyone there?"

Suddenly, Dusty started diving toward Bulldog.

The Sky Cam One reporter exclaimed, "Wait! It's Racer Number Seven, Crophopper, pulling up beside him."

Back in Propwash Junction, the gang was on the edge of their seats. "What's he doing?" Dottie asked.

"Apply your left aileron," Dusty instructed Bulldog. The rest of the pack flew past them, but Dusty didn't care. All he knew was that a fellow racer was about to crash and burn if he didn't help!

"Okay," Bulldog replied, and immediately righted himself. But he was still losing altitude fast.

"Stop roll," Dusty said. "Now quick, pull up."

"Got it," Bulldog said as he and Dusty got closer and closer to the ground.

"Harder . . . harder," Dusty said.

The planes zoomed under a bridge. "Slight roll right," Dusty instructed. Then he looked up to see a castle straight ahead. "Whoa! Castle. *Big* castle. Pull up, hard roll right."

Dusty held his breath as Bulldog weaved his way around the castle spires. "Stop roll," Dusty said.

"Are you still there?" Bulldog asked.

"I'm right here. I'll fly right alongside you," Dusty responded. The fans at home watched nervously as Dusty guided Bulldog along a river to the airport.

The rest of the racers had already landed, with Rip still in first place. A voice over the loudspeaker shouted, "*Achtung!* We have a mayday! Clear the runway!" Emergency vehicles immediately scrambled onto the tarmac.

Up in the air, Dusty and Bulldog were nearing the runway. Dusty knew the landing was going to be tricky. "Add power. Easy, now," he instructed Bulldog. "Good. Flaps down. Lock 'em."

"Careful," El Chupacabra whispered as he watched anxiously from the ground.

"Landing gear down," Dusty said as they approached the runway.

"And locked," Bulldog replied.

"Begin your flare," instructed Dusty, knowing they were seconds from either touching down or crashing. "Power back a little." Then he heard the familiar CHIRP-CHIRP as their tires touched the runway in a perfect landing. Everyone on the ground cheered.

"Touchdown! Nicely done," he said to Bulldog.

The emergency crews rushed forward and began to clean the oil off Bulldog's canopy.

"Thanks for your help, matey," Bulldog said, exhausted. "I couldn't have done it without . . ." When the oil was washed away, Bulldog could see again. "You?" he asked when he saw that Dusty was the one who had guided him in. "*You* saved me? What did I tell you, boy? Every plane for himself, right?"

Dusty shrugged. "Where I come from, if you see someone falling from the sky—"

"Yes, but this is a competition," interrupted Bulldog. "Now you're dead last. And I owe you my life." The tough old racer's eyes welled with tears.

"Are you crying?" Dusty asked.

"I don't cry. I'm British," Bulldog explained, still sniffling. "Thanks, matey."

"Sure thing, Bulldog," Dusty replied as a swarm of reporters rushed over to the barricade near the runway.

"Bulldog! Bulldog! Can we get a few words?" they shouted.

As Bulldog rolled up to the reporters, Rip approached Dusty. "I gotta say, crop duster, you are a nice guy," he said.

"Hey, thanks, Rip," Dusty replied. He still didn't realize that the racer never said anything nice—and meant it.

"And we all know where nice guys finish," Rip added before he rolled off with Ned and Zed. Dusty glanced up at the leaderboard and sighed. He was indeed last.

Later that night, the racers gathered to unwind with drinks at a German oil hall. A waitress set down a mug in front of Dusty. He was feeling pretty low about his current standing in the race. "Dead last," he said to his buddy, El Chupacabra.

"At least you are not last in the race for love," El Chupacabra replied, nearly in tears.

"Rochelle?" asked Dusty.

El Chupacabra nodded solemnly. "Her passion is, sadly, not for me."

"Tough break, El Chu," Dusty said as a little car approached them.

Dusty looked at the stranger curiously. The car smiled bashfully and said, "My name is Franz, and I am a huge fan."

Dusty was shocked.

"I have fans?" he asked.

Franz blinked and said, "Oh, no, no, no. Just me. And I would like to say *danke* for representing all us little planes!

"But you're a car," Dusty said.

"Ja, ja, ja," the little car replied, "but I am what you call a *Flugzeugauto*. One of only six flying cars ever built!" He rolled over to a set of folded wings and clicked them onto himself. The wings swung outward and Franz transformed into a plane.

"Whoa!" exclaimed Dusty. He had never seen such a thing! The little plane said, *"Guten Tag,* Herr Dusty. I am Von Fliegenhosen!"

Dusty looked at him, confused. "Didn't you just say your name was Franz?"

The plane said, *"Nein, nein, nein.* Franz is the guy with no spine who is in charge when we putter about the cobblestones. In the air, *I* am in charge!"

El Chupacabra and Dusty exchanged a look. "This guy needs to get his head gasket checked," El Chu told Dusty. "Serious identity issues."

"This from the one wearing a mask?" Von Fliegenhosen asked.

"Touché!" El Chupacabra replied with a laugh.

Then Von Fliegenhosen changed back into

Franz the car. "We are both pulling for you, Herr Dusty," he said.

"Well, thanks for the support," said Dusty. "I need all the help I can get."

Franz looked Dusty over thoughtfully. "I have a humble suggestion. Would you not be much faster without the pipes and tank and whatnot weighing you down?"

"My sprayer again?" Dusty asked.

"*Ja,*" Franz said, smiling. "Why carry around the extra weight?"

"The little crazy car is right," El Chu agreed. "Perhaps you need to start thinking like a *racer*."

▰▰▰▰▰▰▰

The next day, Dusty underwent a transformation. "This is reversible, right? You're being careful down there, right?" he asked the mechanics as his crop-dusting parts were removed. "Whoa! Oh, that's cold!"

A little while later, he rolled down the runway looking sleek and feeling like a new plane. He even had some new racing stripes. "So, what do you think?" Dusty asked Franz and El Chu.

"Zippy stripes!" Franz said excitedly.

"*¡Fantástico!*" El Chu agreed. "It is freeing, yes?"

"You took the words right out of my mouth," replied Dusty. Then he, Franz, and El Chu took off and circled the airfield. Dusty was thrilled. He was flying faster than he ever had before!

Soon Dusty and the other racers took to the sky for the third leg of the rally, which would take them from Germany to India. Dusty finally had the edge he needed, and quickly rose in the standings.

Colin Cowling reported Dusty's surprising turnaround to racing fans around the world. "The real story here is Dusty Crophopper," he said. "He is passing one flier after another."

Brent Mustangburger shared Colin's excitement, adding, "That's right. This guy was built to dust crops, but he's dusting the competition!"

As the racers flew over Dubai toward India, fans all over the world were rooting for Dusty—their favorite underdog!

The racers were soon flying over India, and the gang from Propwash Junction was gathered around the television, watching every minute. Things were looking up for Dusty, and they didn't want to miss a thing!

"This could be Crophopper's leg all the way," Colin said. "The racers will have to fly under a hard ceiling of one thousand feet. Stay under the clouds and in the hills."

Flying low was what Dusty did best. He weaved through the hills, passing racer after racer.

By the time they landed at the air base in Agra, Dusty had moved all the way up to eighth place!

The reporters ignored Ripslinger and crowded around Dusty. "Why are they wasting their time with him?" Rip asked Ned and Zed angrily. "He's a tractor with wings."

Zed shrugged. "Actually, it's really a compelling underdog story. It's like *Rocky*!"

"It's more like David and Goliath!" said Ned.

"Or *Old Yeller*," Zed added.

"That's not an underdog story!" Ned protested.

"There's a dog in it," Zed told him smugly.

"Enough!" Rip snapped, ending their debate. "Soon we'll be overrun by every banner tower, skywriter, and air freighter who thinks they can be one of us! That farm boy forgot who he is and where he came from. He's not about to stop me from making history."

Rip suddenly got a serious look on his face—like he was deep in thought. Ned and Zed knew that when Rip got that look, there was going to be trouble.

In the meantime, the reporters still couldn't get enough of Dusty. "Where did you learn to race?" one of them asked.

"From my coach, Skipper," Dusty replied. "He's the reason I'm even here. He's an amazing instructor. And a great friend. He flew dozens of missions all over the world. And I'm sure if he could, he'd be with us right now."

Back in Propwash Junction, Skipper was watching Dusty's interview on the television. His student's words got him thinking. Maybe it was time to try something he hadn't done in a long time.

CHAPTER 18

Later that night, Skipper peeked outside his hangar door to make sure the coast was clear, then gave Sparky a nod. The little tug pushed him onto the moonlit runway, then rolled off to the side.

Skipper took a deep breath. While Sparky watched hopefully, the old fighter started his engine and inched forward. But within seconds, he gave up and shut down again.

Sparky rushed over to him. "Whoa, your engine sounds kinda rough. Must be a mag misfire." He was trying to give Skipper an excuse for not being able to fly—and Skipper knew it. The old war hero said nothing as Sparky towed him back to the hangar.

The next morning, it was business as usual in Propwash Junction as Chug busily sold his Dusty

Crophopper souvenirs. A customer rolled up to the table and asked, "Hey, you got anything new?"

"Glad you asked," Chug replied. "I'm now selling these one-of-a-kind Dusty commemorative mugs." Chug demonstrated the cup's working propeller. He could see the delight in the fan's eyes and knew he'd made another sale.

Just then, the radio in the corner squawked, "This is Dusty Crophopper calling Propwash Junction, over."

"I'll be back in ten," Chug said. Soon he, Dottie, Skipper, and Sparky were all gathered around the radio. "Dusty! Eighth place. You finally removed your M 5000!" Dottie said.

Chug looked confused. "His what?"

"His Microair 5000 DL Aerial Applicator," Dottie explained.

But Chug was only more confused. "Use your words," he said.

"His sprayer!" Dottie cried exasperatedly.

Skipper spoke into the radio. "Got a big leg tomorrow," he said. "How you feelin'?"

"I can't believe it! The mighty Himalayas!" chimed in Chug.

Dottie seemed concerned. "Dusty, that vertical wind shear is going to be wicked over those mountains."

Chug nodded. "Good thing about being that high up, there's not a lot of oxygen. So if you crash, no explosion!"

"Great," Dusty replied without enthusiasm.

Chug grinned. "Of course, you could die of hypothermia. Or an avalanche could get ya. Then of course there's pneumonia, or even frostbite."

"Chug, Chug, I got it," Dusty said, sighing. Telling him all the ways he could meet with disaster was not helping! "Skip, what if a guy wanted to fly through the mountains instead of over them?"

"Bad idea," Skipper warned Dusty. His tone was serious. "The Wrenches flew through terrain like that in the Assault of Kunming. And Dottie's right, wind comin' over the peaks can stir up rotors that'll drag you right down. You can fly a whole lot higher than you think."

Dusty sighed. He was afraid Skipper was going to say that.

"Roger that," Dusty replied, still wondering how he could take the mountains at a low altitude.

Dusty clicked off the radio and saw Rochelle roll by, followed by El Chu. *"¡Hola, corazón!"* El Chu called to her. "Are you tired? Because you have been flying through my mind nonstop."

Rochelle turned to him. "Why would I be tired flying through such a teeny, tiny space?"

As she rolled off, El Chupacabra called to her, "Ah! You can only pretend for so long." Then he looked at Dusty with a pained expression. "I am Icarus and she is the sun. I fly too close, and I melt," he said sadly.

"Maybe you're trying too hard," Dusty suggested, as if he was an expert at romance. "Look, all you gotta do is go over, open your mouth, and say—"

"Hello," said Ishani. The Indian racer seemed to have appeared out of nowhere.

Dusty jumped. His cool vanished. El Chu could see Dusty had a crush on Ishani and wanted to give them some time alone. He pretended he had to leave.

Ishani smiled and said, "I want to compliment you on your success, Dusty. You're doing very well for your first race."

"That means a lot coming from you," Dusty answered. "I mean, c'mon, you were named Most

Aerodynamic Racer! And let me just say, you are *so* aerodynamic!"

They shared a smile as a mooing tractor rolled by. "What's with all the tractors around here?" Dusty asked.

"They're sacred," Ishani replied. "Many believe that we will be recycled as tractors."

"Oh? Well, I believe in recycling," Dusty said eagerly.

Ishani smiled. "Have you ever been to the Taj Mahal?" she asked.

"No, I haven't," Dusty replied. Before he knew it, Ishani was whisking him off to see one of India's most famous landmarks.

"Must be nice to be back home," Dusty said as they flew together.

"It's complicated," she told Dusty. "I have a billion fans. They're all expecting me to win."

"Maybe this time you will," Dusty replied.

They arrived at the Taj Mahal just as the sun was beginning to set. Dusty was dazzled by its incredible beauty. The white marble walls and towers reflected the golden sunlight, making it sparkle like a jewel. "Wow," Dusty said. "This place is amazing!"

"It really is," agreed Ishani. "And tomorrow you'll fly over the magnificent Himalayas."

Dusty tried not to show his apprehension. "Those little hills? Yeah, no big deal."

Ishani nodded. "You like to fly low, don't you?" she asked.

Dusty fidgeted a bit. "Oh, that? That's uh—strategic. Air density and combustion."

Ishani chuckled. "You know, you could follow the Iron Compass instead."

"Iron Compass?" Dusty asked.

Ishani nodded. "Railroad tracks through a valley in the mountains. So you can still fly low."

Dusty was thrilled. Now he could fly through the mountains instead of over them, just as he had hoped. "Really? Thanks, Ishani," he said. He smiled happily as they watched the sun set together.

CHAPTER 19

The next day, it was time for the racers to tackle the fourth leg of the rally.

"Every racer's nightmare is scaling the Himalayas," Brent Mustangburger announced. "It's a short leg ahead, but extremely treacherous."

Dusty looked at the enormous snow-covered peaks that stood between him and his destination in Nepal and was grateful all over again for Ishani's advice. He broke off from the rest of the racers and quickly found the railroad tracks she had told him about. He followed them as they curved through the mountains—but eventually the path got narrower and narrower, and the peaks on either side got taller and taller. He peered through the falling snow and saw something straight ahead. It was a tunnel!

Dusty panicked and pulled up, up, up toward the

mountaintops, but the altitude quickly made him feel dizzy and sick. He realized he had only two choices: Go over the mountain or go through it. *Over* was not an option, so Dusty clenched his teeth, dived down, and headed right for the mouth of the dark tunnel. He was going through it!

Once inside, Dusty's wingtips scraped against the rock walls, creating a shower of sparks in his wake. But the worst was yet to come. Dusty saw a pinpoint of light up ahead and heard an ominous TOOOOOOOT! It was an oncoming train! He gunned it, hoping to beat the train before it barreled into the tunnel on the other side. With his wingtips scraping up even more sparks, Dusty gave it everything he had.

A little while later, as if in a dream, Dusty floated through some puffy white clouds before touching down on a dirt runway. Several old mini-truck monks greeted him. "Uh . . . hello?" Dusty said, bewildered. "Is this where I'm supposed to be?"

"That is one of life's great questions," a monk replied.

Dusty remembered being in the tunnel and gasped, "I'm dead!"

Just then, a local race official rolled up. "Mr. Crophopper. Welcome to Nepal."

"I don't understand," Dusty said. "Have the others left already?"

The official replied, "Actually, no one else is here yet. You're in first place."

Dusty was stunned. *"Really?"*

It wasn't long before the other racers landed and Ripslinger got the news. "He flew through a *what?*" Rip yelled. Ned and Zed cowered. They could see Ripslinger's anger building.

Reporters swarmed around Dusty, shouting their questions. "Dusty, how does it feel to be in first place?"

Dusty grinned. "It feels great. But more than anything, I'm just happy I fit through that tunnel." Then Dusty saw Ishani across the tarmac. "Excuse me, guys," he said, and rolled over to see her.

"Crazy day today, huh?" Dusty asked.

Ishani seemed uneasy. "Yeah. A very exciting win for you today," she replied. "Quite a risk you took."

Dusty nodded. Then he noticed something. "Hey, your propeller? Is it new?"

"Oh, I suppose it is," Ishani replied casually.

"A Skyslycer Mark 5, right?" Dusty asked. "Aren't those made exclusively for Ripslinger's race team?" Dusty suddenly understood what was going on. Ishani was helping Rip. She had sent Dusty through the mountains so that Rip could beat him. Her new propeller was the proof.

Ishani quickly looked away. "Uh, are they?"

"Yeah, they are," Dusty told her. "You set me up."

"It's complicated, okay?" she said. "I really thought that you'd just turn around."

"Well, you were wrong. And I was wrong about you," Dusty said. Then he rolled past Ripslinger and said, "Oh, hey, Rip. Thanks for first place."

From Nepal, the rally continued with its fifth leg over the vast country of China. As the competitors weaved through rice paddies and over the Great Wall, the Chinese race fans cheered them on.

"Flying low and quick, Dusty Crophopper is managing to hold on to the top spot," Brent Mustangburger said. "But current reigning champ Ripslinger is just seconds behind him. This surprise battle for first place has made Dusty Crophopper the one to watch."

All around the globe, working-class vehicles were following Dusty's progress in the race and cheering him on.

By the time the racers landed at Shanghai Pudong International Airport, Ripslinger was fuming. He couldn't stand that Dusty was getting the worldwide attention that was supposed to be his. When he saw

Zed watching clips of Dusty on a tablet computer, he smashed the screen.

Zed protested, but Rip just shrugged. "A new one's comin' out in two weeks," he said.

In another part of the airport, Dusty sat alone by the radio, talking to Skipper. "You're really showin' them big-time racers a thing or two, huh?" his coach said.

"Yeah, we head out across the Pacific tomorrow, Skip," Dusty radioed back. "You were stationed there for a while, right? Got any advice?"

"Back in 'forty-one, during the Battle of Wake Island, the Wrenches ran into serious monsoons with embedded CBs that could tear your wings right off," Skipper replied. "Be careful."

Dusty knew about CBs. They were cumulonimbus clouds—tall and thick and famous for being able to create really dangerous weather.

"And one more thing . . . ," Skipper said. "I'm proud of you, Dusty."

"Thanks, wingman," Dusty replied. Skipper's words meant a lot to him.

Just then, Dottie's voice came over the radio. "Hey, Dusty, we have a surprise for you!"

Chug could barely contain himself. "Oh, ya gotta let me tell him!" he said. But Chug was so excited, he couldn't seem to remember what the surprise was. "Um, oh . . . I know it. It's on the tip of my tongue. I'll remember!"

Dottie tried to help him out. "We're going . . . ," she began.

Chug nodded and repeated, "We're going . . ."

"To . . . ," Dottie said.

"To . . . ," repeated Chug.

"Mmmmmmmm . . . ," Dottie said, hoping she'd given him enough of a hint.

"Mmmmmmmmmalaysia!" cried Chug.

"Mexico!" Dottie corrected, rolling her eyes.

Chug beamed. "Mexico! That's it! We're gonna meet you in Mexico!"

"Really?" Dusty replied.

"Yep. Tickets are on Sparky and me!" Chug said proudly. "We sold three hundred and twenty-six Dusty bobbleheads, one hundred and forty-three antenna balls, two hundred and three spinner mugs—"

"And," Sparky announced as he rolled into the hangar covered from top to bottom in Dusty

Crophopper souvenirs, "one thousand whistles! Go Team Dusterino! Yeah!"

"You sure you're up for it, Skipper?" Dusty asked.

Skipper smiled. "You bet. Somebody else is doing the flying."

Dusty was thrilled. "That's great news, guys! I'll see you in Mexico!" Dusty rolled off happily, thinking one hop across the Pacific and he'd be with his Propwash buddies again. Then he saw El Chupacabra roll by with a wild look in his eyes.

"Hey, El Chu, where's the fire?" Dusty asked.

The masked plane stopped and said, "It is in my soul! Tonight I shall win the heart of Miss Rochelle." Dusty watched his friend position himself beneath Rochelle's balcony and plug in a boom box. Then El Chu belted out what he thought was a romantic song while a driving disco beat blasted through the speakers.

Rochelle looked out from her balcony, annoyed by the noise. "No, no, no! A thousand nos!" she called down to him, and slammed her door.

El Chu was going to give it another try, but the music abruptly stopped. He looked over and saw

Dusty holding the plug to the boom box. *"¿Que pasó, Dusty? What are you doing?"*

Dusty signaled, and several mariachi tugs rolled up, playing their guitars in a gentle rhythm. Then Dusty lit some candles to create a romantic mood. "Low and slow," Dusty advised. El Chu got the idea. He smiled and started to sing again, but this time he softly crooned the words instead of belting them.

Rochelle peeked out, charmed by his new approach. *"Buenas noches, querida,"* El Chupacabra said smoothly.

Rochelle answered sweetly in French.

El Chu leaned toward Dusty. "What does that mean?" he asked.

"No idea," Dusty replied, "but French Canadian is the language of love . . . in Canada . . . so it's gotta be good."

El Chu smiled. "I am in your debt, compadre. If ever you need me, I shall be there!"

"Compadre," said Dusty. "I like that."

The next morning, the racers lined up for the next leg of the rally. The competitors would be flying to Mexico, with a fuel stop in Hawaii. Dusty was currently in first place in the rally, and Rip was in second.

"You are looking live at Shanghai Pudong International Airport," Brent Mustangburger said, "witnessing one of the greatest competitions ever in the Wings Around The Globe Rally."

As Rip glared at the leaderboard, Dusty rolled up, grinning. "First place. Not too bad for a farm boy!" he said.

Ripslinger seethed even more. He couldn't believe Dusty was ahead of him!

Meanwhile, El Chu was hurrying to the starting line. He looked harried and a bit of a mess.

"What happened to you?" Dusty asked.

"That song," El Chu said, "it flipped a switch."

Dusty turned to see Rochelle chasing after El Chu. It was obvious that she was wildly in love with him. She grabbed his cape and pulled at him. "My little monster! Come here!" she shouted.

"She is like a jaguar now!" El Chu whimpered as Rochelle dragged him away with her.

"Start your engines!" announced the official, and soon the racers were heading out over the Pacific. Surrounded by patchy fog, they passed Chinese junks as the coastline disappeared beneath them.

"This is our sixth and longest leg," Brent Mustangburger said. "These racers will need to follow their GPS antennas because there's a big ocean between here and Mexico."

The pack climbed into the clouds, and Dusty stayed in his usual low position. Just then, Zed appeared in the fog behind him, zoomed up alongside Dusty, and in one swift move broke off his GPS antenna.

"No!" Dusty shouted as he helplessly watched the antenna fall. He circled, not knowing what to do. All the other racers had disappeared into the clouds above him. Dusty could hear their engines fading, and he realized he was completely alone. Worst of all, without his antenna, he had no idea which direction he was flying in. "Hawaii, are you there? Do you read? I am low on fuel," he radioed. But there was only silence.

Dusty strained to see the glow of the sun through the fog. It was the only marker he could locate in an endless ocean, and he zoomed toward it.

A little while later, Dusty heard an alarm go off on his control panel. He was running out of fuel! His hopes were sinking fast when a navy fighter jet named Bravo suddenly appeared out of the mist next to him. "Unknown rider. Unknown rider," his voice boomed. "You have entered restricted airspace. Why haven't you responded to radio contact?"

"Somebody cut off my antenna," Dusty replied.

"Identify yourself," Bravo said.

"I'm Dusty Crophopper," answered Dusty.

"Roger that," Bravo said, and then radioed his ship. "Bogey has been identified as Crophopper Seven."

"I'm running on vapors. I need to land!" Dusty cried, desperation in his voice.

Another fighter jet, Echo, pulled up alongside

Dusty. "What are you doing out here with an empty tank?" he asked.

"I thought I'd refuel in Hawaii, but—" began Dusty.

"What? Hawaii is three hundred seventy-five miles southwest of here," Bravo told him.

"Listen, Crophopper," Echo said, "better follow us to the boat. No bingo fields around here."

"Bingo fields?" Dusty asked, confused.

"Places to land," Echo told him.

Dusty soon discovered that the "boat" he would be landing on was the *Dwight D. Flysenhower*— Skipper's old aircraft carrier!

CHAPTER 22

The two jets escorted Dusty toward the ship and radioed their squadron to get ready for an emergency landing.

"That's all I need," said the captain to the control pitty, "a civilian exploding on my deck."

"We could rig the barricade, sir," the control pitty suggested.

"All engines ahead flank," replied the captain.

The deckhands quickly moved a barricade of thick nylon netting to the end of the flight deck. It was there to catch Dusty in case he overshot the runway.

Bravo and Echo lined Dusty up with the barricade on the ship. "All you gotta do is throttle on back," Bravo told Dusty.

"I'm not sure I can do this," Dusty replied nervously.

"I don't see how you have a choice," said Echo.

"But that runway is *moving*," Dusty protested.

"We'll set you up on the glide path," replied Echo.

"Runways are not supposed to move!" insisted Dusty.

Echo and Bravo could see that Dusty was in a full panic, and they tried to talk him through it. "Slow down . . . take it easy . . . throttle on back . . ."

There was no turning back as Dusty approached his moving target. His wheels hit the deck with one giant bounce, and he landed in the barricade. Everyone cheered as the LSO announced, "We gotcha Crophopper!"

The crew had been following the Wings Around The Globe Rally!

"Come on," Bravo said to Dusty. "Let's get you fixed up, refueled, and back in the race. You are way behind."

Dusty rolled into an elevator with Bravo and Echo. "Thanks, guys. You saved my tail out there." They got out at the hangar deck and Dusty found himself looking at a wall filled with photos, names, and medals.

"Hey, what is that?" Dusty asked.

"That's the Jolly Wrenches Wall of Fame," explained Bravo.

"Every flier, every mission!" Echo added.

Dusty scanned the wall, looking for Skipper. "There he is," he said. There was only one mission listed for his coach: Glendalcanal. Dusty was confused. "But I don't understand. Why is there only one mission?" he wondered aloud.

※※※※※※※※※

Back in Propwash Junction, the gang was preparing to board a cargo plane heading for Mexico. They couldn't wait to meet up with Dusty! Chug was the last to board. He was lugging so much baggage, it was slowing him down.

"What's all that?" Dottie asked him.

"Well, I've never been out of the country," explained Chug.

Dottie pointed out that they were only going to be in Mexico for two days.

"Gotta be prepared, right?" Chug told her. "Got beachwear, dinnerwear, underwear, got my floaties . . ."

But before Chug could finish, the radio in the hangar went off. It was Dusty calling. "Skipper? Come in, Skipper!"

"Dusty!" Skipper answered. "We're headin' off to Mexico right now. Glad ya got there safe. Weather report says a major storm is brewin' out there."

"I'm not in Mexico," Dusty said as the navy pitties replaced his antenna and fueled him up. "I'm with the Jolly Wrenches."

Skipper was speechless for a moment. "You're on the *Flysenhower*?" he asked uneasily.

"Hey, I saw the Wall of Fame," Dusty continued. "They only list one mission for you."

Skipper took a deep breath and shifted uncomfortably. He didn't want to talk about the days with his old squadron, and tried to steer the conversation in a different direction. What mattered most to Skipper now was getting Dusty through a dangerous patch of weather. "Dusty, if you're not past that storm yet, you need to—"

Dusty interrupted him. He couldn't take his mind off what he'd seen on the wall. "That can't be right. It must be a mistake."

Skipper kept talking about the storm. "Look,

you've gotta get outta there. You're gonna have to *fly high*."

But Dusty wouldn't let it go. "Is it true?" he asked him.

"Listen to me, get above the storm—"

"Skipper! Is it true?" Dusty tried again.

"It's true," his coach finally said.

Dusty was stunned. "But all those stories?" he said, hurt and confused.

Just then, the chief petty pitty rolled in. "Crophopper, we've got weather moving in fast. You've got to take off before it's too late."

"I just a need a second here," Dusty said, waiting for Skipper's reply.

But the chief petty pitty shut down the transmission. "That's a negative, son! You don't go now, you don't go at all."

In no time, Dusty found himself on the deck in the driving rain. Loudspeakers blared an urgent warning of an oncoming cyclone!

The storm clouds were growing darker as the crew readied Dusty to be launched off the deck in what looked like a giant slingshot. A shooter tug instructed Dusty to report to Catapult Two.

"The cat'll take ya from zero to one hundred sixty knots in two seconds," he said.

"We're gonna check your weight and set the steam pressure," another shooter tug told him.

"Remember, climb straight ahead once ya get airborne. Get above the storm," added the first shooter.

Dusty was so distracted and shaken by the idea that Skipper had lied to him that he barely heard the instructions. Then Echo said, "Okay. Engine full throttle, nod to the shooter when you're set."

"Go win it for the Wrenches, Dusty!" shouted Bravo. *Volo Pro Veritas.*

"Headwinds good," another shooter said. "Pressure is good. Go on Cat Two." He saluted, pointed the catapult forward, and with a WHOOSH! Dusty was launched off the deck. In seconds, he was alone in the clouds.

That night over the Pacific, Dusty was just a speck against a dark, open ocean. Thunder rumbled overhead, but all Dusty could think about was Skipper. "How can it be only one mission?" he muttered to himself.

He could hear Skipper's voice in his head talking about the Battle of Airway, the raid in Tujunga Harbor, the Aleutians, the Battle of Wake Island, and the Assault on Kunming.

The storm bore down on him with brutal force. Torrential rain pinged against his fuselage while thunder threatened to split open the sky. Lightning zigzagged across his path. He was struggling to dodge the churning waves just below him when a huge swell came up and drenched him. His engine began to cough and sputter, and he found himself arcing downward.

"Mayday, mayday, mayday!" he cried. "I am going down! Eighteen degrees north, six minutes, one hundred nineteen degrees . . ."

As Dusty hit the water, he felt his landing gear crack and his wings buckle. Then another wave rolled over him, covered his wings, and began to pull him down. "Help!" Dusty called frantically as he disappeared into the cold gray sea.

CHAPTER 24

All the other racers had arrived at the airport in Mexico hours before. Reporters surrounded Ripslinger, asking him for information. "Señor Ripslinger," one said, "do you have any comment on the disappearance of Dusty Crophopper?"

"Dusty was a nice guy who flew the challenge and pierced the clouds of mediocrity. We're all gonna miss him," he said.

After he was out of earshot of the reporters, he turned to Ned and Zed and added with a snicker, "Let's hope he makes a better boat than a plane!"

"That was a good one, boss," Ned said.

An angry El Chu rolled up to Rip. "Señor Dusty has ten times the engine you do!" he exclaimed.

"And ten times the integrity!" Ishani added.

"Said the plane with the shiny new propeller,"

Rip sneered. "How much integrity did that one cost you, sweetheart?"

"Too much!" Ishani replied. "You used to be a great champion. How the mighty have fallen."

<hr/>

Meanwhile, a Mexican navy helicopter had heard Dusty's radio pleas for help. It rushed to the scene and dropped a net into the water. Dusty was aware of being hauled out of the waves just before he blacked out.

Later that night, reporters' cameras flashed as the helicopter gently lowered a battered Dusty onto the tarmac in Mexico. Dusty's worried friends rushed over and brought him inside the medical hangar.

"Broken wing ribs, twisted gear, bent prop," Dottie said as she inspected Dusty's injuries. She shook her head and sighed. "And your main spar is cracked . . . bad. It's over."

Dusty could see from his friends' faces that they were completely devastated. But there was only one thing on his mind. He looked at Skipper and said, "One mission? So much for *Volo Pro Veritas*."

The gang glanced at each other, confused by

Dusty's remark. Skipper cleared his throat and said, "Can we get a minute alone, please?" He looked down at his faithful tug. "You too, Sparky."

Skipper took a deep breath and sighed wearily. "My first patrol as a Jolly Wrench was at Glendalcanal," he said. His memory drifted back to World War II, when he was the leader of the young, brash Jolly Wrenches. "My squadron was all rookies, all razor-sharp. I should know. I trained every single one of 'em. It was supposed to be a routine patrol. A milk run."

Skipper recalled that he and his squadron were scanning the skies for action over the Pacific. A hole in the clouds opened up, and they saw what they thought was a single enemy supply ship.

"Easy pickin's," said one of Skipper's students. "Whaddaya say?"

"Negative," Skipper told him. "Our orders are to recon and report back."

"Come on, Skip. It'll be a turkey shoot!" another rookie said.

Skipper gave in. "All right," he told them. "Let's go in for a closer look."

But when the squadron broke through the clouds,

instead of a single ship, Skipper and his young fliers were faced with an entire fleet. It was too late to pull back up. The enemy had seen them. Seconds later, Skipper's squadron was engulfed in antiaircraft fire.

The Jolly Wrenches fought back, but they were outnumbered. Skipper bitterly remembered his newly trained rookies falling from the sky all around him.

Skipper was hit and went tumbling into the ocean. Later, a rescue ship came by and pulled him out of the water.

"My whole squadron . . . under my command," Skipper said sorrowfully. He remembered the awful moment when the medic told him he was the only survivor. "After that, I just couldn't bring myself to fly again."

Dusty just stared at him, trying to take it all in.

"Let me ask you something," Skipper continued. "If you knew the truth about my past, would you have asked me to train you?"

Dusty slumped. He didn't know how to respond, so he just turned and rolled out of the hanger.

"I'm sorry, Dusty," Skipper said softly.

The following day, everyone was getting ready for the final leg of the race to New York. But Dusty stayed in his hangar, sad and alone. Dottie took a deep breath and approached him. "Dusty?" she whispered.

"Can you believe it?" Dusty asked, barely looking at her. "He hasn't been straight with me this whole time. At least you were honest. You said I wasn't built for this. I guess I shoulda listened to you."

Dottie rolled around to face him. "Dusty, if you had listened to me, I'd never, ever forgive myself. Look, the Skipper may have been wrong for what he did, but he was right about you. You're a racer, and now the whole world knows it."

Dusty was touched. "Thanks, that means a lot," he said. "But I've gone as far as I can go. I'm busted up. Look at me."

Just then, El Chupacabra appeared in the hangar

doorway. "Dusty, I cannot bear the thought of competing without you." Then he rolled in a cart with a pair of wings on it.

"Those are the wings of a T-33 Shooting Star," Dusty said in amazement.

El Chu nodded. "When the great Mexican Air Force needed help, American T-33s came. They did not ask questions. They did not hesitate. They were there because that is what compadres do."

Dusty looked at a metal box next to the wings. "And what's that?" he asked.

"That is my lunch," El Chu explained. "Don't touch! But the wings are yours."

"El Chu, I really appreciate—" Dusty began, trying to thank him. But the macho masked plane stopped him.

"¡Silencio!" El Chu ordered. "After all, you helped me with my pursuits of the heart. Now we are here to help you."

"We?" Dusty asked, looking around.

"Oui," Rochelle said as she and the rest of the racers gathered around with carts full of parts for Dusty. "Good luck tomorrow, Dusty. I'm so proud to compete with you."

Bulldog nodded heartily. "You're a good egg, Dusty. Here's a sat-nav device, just in case . . . in case you ever find yourself lost without a friend to help you through it," he said, choking back the tears.

More racers followed, offering what they had:

"Here's a flow-control valve."

"How about a starter generator?"

"Got a brand-new master cylinder here for you."

They all were honored to be racing beside Dusty—once just a fellow racer, now a friend.

Dusty was overwhelmed. "Thanks, everyone," he told them.

Dottie was beaming. "This is fantastic!" she said, checking out the new parts. "Looks like all we need now is—"

"A new propeller?" Ishani asked. "How about a Skyslycer Mark 5?" She pushed over her own propeller on a cart.

Dusty was confused. "But that's your propeller. You could still win the race."

Ishani smiled. "Oh, I intend to," she said, "but with my old propeller. This one didn't really suit me, but I think you will have a lot better luck with it."

"Thanks, Ishani," Dusty said, smiling. Then he

turned to Dottie. "Can you fix me?" he asked.

Dottie grinned. "Does a PT6A have a multistage compressor?" she asked enthusiastically.

Everyone looked at each other blankly. They had no idea what she was talking about.

Dottie rolled her eyes. "Yes!" she told them. "Yes, it does!"

The racers cheered, and Dottie shouted to the other tugs, "All right, you guys, let's get him ready to race!"

A little while later, Dottie and the other teams' mechanics began repairing Dusty. As they worked into the night, Chug watched highlights from Rip's previous races. Something caught Chug's eye, and he went back and watched it again. A smile slowly spread across his face as he realized something that had gone unnoticed by everyone. He quickly told Dusty, who listened with astonishment.

CHAPTER 26

The next morning, the racers rolled out for the final leg of the rally. Fitted with sleek, streamlined wings and all the latest gleaming technology, Dusty looked like a different plane. He looked like—a racer!

"We'll see you in New York," Dottie told him as he passed her, Chug, and Sparky on the way to the tarmac. Skipper wasn't there. He had decided it would be best if he didn't join the others.

Onlookers stared at Dusty in disbelief. "He's back!" one of them shouted.

Ripslinger snorted. "You've gotta be kidding me."

"Whoa!" Zed said when he laid eyes on Dusty. "Who's that guy?"

"It's the crop duster," Ned told him.

"Another one?" Zed asked.

"It's the same one, knucklehead!" Ned snapped.

Rip lost patience with them both. "Move aside, idiots," he said. Ripslinger rolled into Dusty's path and blocked his way. "Bolting on a few new parts doesn't change who you are," Rip said with a sneer. He revved his prop menacingly. "I can still smell the farm on you."

Dusty thought for a moment, then grinned. "Oh, you know what?" he said. "I finally get it. You're afraid of getting beat by a crop duster."

Dusty pushed forward, revving his engine, until Rip had no choice but to back up. "Well, check six. 'Cause I'm coming."

After Dusty rolled off, Ripslinger turned to Ned and Zed. "We're going to end this once and for all," he told them. He had no idea that Skipper was listening from a hangar nearby.

The racers lined up for takeoff. "This one's all about speed and the willingness to give it all," Brent Mustangburger said. "First to cut the ribbon in New York takes home the trophy and the glory."

The race pitty dropped his wing, and Rip roared off the starting line. "And we're off as the first fliers take to the air!" Brent shouted.

One by one, the other racers departed. "The rest of the field is now off and running," Brent continued. "Though Crophopper did not complete the previous leg, race officials ruled that his radio had been tampered with. So he'll be allowed to compete—but with a severe time penalty."

Dusty pulled up to the starting line alone, and the crowd counted down the clock to his takeoff time. *"Cinco . . . cuatro . . . tres . . . dos . . . uno!"*

When the clock hit zero, Dusty roared down the runway and blasted into the sky!

Dusty zoomed across the sky, passing racer after racer. As the pack approached the Sierra Madre Mountains, he stayed low and watched the shadows of the planes above him—then made his move and sailed right past them, moving up to sixth place.

"Good show, Dusty!" Bulldog called out as Dusty passed below him.

The racers flew over the Rio Grande—the narrow river between Mexico and the United States—and El Chu and Rochelle jockeyed for position. But below, Dusty passed them both. He was approaching Deadstick Desert at lightning speed.

Ripslinger, Ned, and Zed were still in the lead as they roared over the barren landscape. Zed glanced back nervously and said, "Um, boss?"

"What?" asked Rip.

"He's here," Zed said.

Rip looked behind and below, and there was Dusty, kicking up sand and coming up fast. "Ugghh!" Rip said in frustration. "Okay. We're out of camera range. You know what to do."

Rip, Ned, and Zed turned and dived toward Dusty.

"Hey, farmer!" cried Zed.

"Time to plow the fields!" Ned yelled.

Rip dropped his landing gear and closed in on Dusty from above. He forced Dusty lower until his wheels smashed into a cactus.

Rip laughed. "Looks like you've run outta airspace, Crophopper."

Rip was right. Dusty was heading straight for a rocky outcropping. He couldn't pull up because Rip was blocking him from above. There was no way out.

But just then, a flash of blue-gray came streaking toward them. It was Skipper! He dived at Rip and forced him away from Dusty.

Dusty pulled up hard to avoid the rocks while Ned and Zed took off in opposite directions.

"Skipper? Whoa! You're flying!" Dusty said. He couldn't believe it.

"You noticed," replied Skipper. "Listen, I got Rip. You take care of the other two."

Ned and Zed were back on Dusty's tail.

"They're on your six, kid!" Skipper warned. "You gotta lose them! Pull hard right! I'll brake left and take out Rip. Use the rocks!"

Dusty knife-edged through a chasm, and when Ned and Zed tried to follow, they collided and got caught between the rocks.

"Yeah!" Dusty cried triumphantly.

Meanwhile, Skipper used the tip of his wing to flip Ripslinger over and send him tumbling across the sky. But Rip wasn't about to lose the race because of an upstart crop duster and a beat-up Corsair. While Skipper checked up on Dusty, Rip tore into the old fighter's tail with his prop.

"No!" Dusty yelled.

"That's why they call 'em Sky*slycers*!" Rip called, laughing, as he headed for the horizon.

Dusty pulled up alongside Skipper. "Are you okay?" he asked.

Skipper turned to him with a big grin. "You kiddin'? I'm great!"

Dusty could see that Skipper had taken some real

damage. "But what about your tail?" Dusty asked.

Skipper laughed. "I'll live," he said. "Go get him! Go!"

Dusty nodded, gritted his teeth, and gunned it.

Ripslinger was confidently zooming over the Mississippi. He didn't know that a mile behind him, Dusty was flying with focus in his eyes, getting closer and closer with every second.

"We're closing in on the final stretch, folks," Colin Cowling announced.

"That's right," added Brent Mustangburger, "and ever since they emerged from Deadstick Desert, Ripslinger has maintained a lead."

At JFK, pitties had their binoculars trained on the empty horizon.

"Any sign of 'em?" the race official asked.

"Nothing yet," another pitty replied.

❌❌❌❌❌❌❌

As the racers crossed the Appalachian Mountains, Dusty was right on Rip's tail. For one fleeting moment, Dusty was even able to pull up alongside him! But then Rip revved his engine and left Dusty behind. "Arrgh!" Dusty yelled in frustration.

Dusty was starting to feel the shadow of defeat overtake him when he looked up. High above, the clouds that looked like streets were forming. "Tailwinds like nothin' you've ever flown," he remembered Skipper saying.

But he also remembered how sick he'd felt the day he tried to reach those clouds. He knew it was time to make a decision. He took a deep breath and swallowed hard. "Roger that, Skip," he said. He squeezed his eyes shut and pulled his nose up, pouring on the power.

The ground quickly disappeared beneath Dusty as he roared into the sky. He kept his eyes shut while he climbed higher and higher. The clouds were getting closer. "Don't look down," he kept telling himself over and over. But he couldn't resist cracking his eyes open for just a second. When he saw how high up he was, panic washed over him. This time, though, he forced himself to keep going.

Finally, he punched through the clouds and, to his complete surprise, was rocketed forward by a gale-force tailwind. "Whoa!" Dusty howled with delight. "Yeah! Whooo!"

He blazed across the entire state of Pennsylvania, riding the wave of wind. He would be approaching New York and the finish line in minutes. Rip was rapidly approaching the city, too, totally oblivious that Dusty was gaining on him from up above.

Dusty finally caught up to Rip and began to dive. . . .

Hundreds of planes, cars, and trucks were filled with anticipation as they waited at JFK to witness the end of the most exciting race in aviation history. Finally, they heard a faint roar in the distance. It got louder and louder, and soon the crowd was able to see the first racer on the horizon.

Ripslinger smiled confidently. His fourth Wings Around The Globe Rally win was seconds away! But Rip couldn't see what the crowd was seeing. It was Dusty, with a look of fierce determination in his eyes.

"Wait a second," Colin announced. "It's Dusty Crophopper!"

The Propwash gang watched breathlessly from the tarmac. "Yes!" Dottie cried.

"Go!" Chug shouted.

"And here they come, down the stretch," Brent Mustangburger said. "It's going to be close. It's anyone's race."

Rip, still thinking he'd left Dusty far behind, glanced to the right and saw the reporters and their cameras. He smiled his usual arrogant grin and tilted toward them. "Get my good side, fellas," he told them.

This was the move Chug had seen in the highlight reel. Rip did it in every race. Dusty knew it was his chance. He swerved left, gave it all he had, and pulled past Rip in the final seconds. Dusty passed Ripslinger and cut the ribbon across the finish line.

"He's done it! He's done it!" screamed Brent Mustangburger.

"From last to first, from obscurity to immortality, the racing world will never forget this day!" Colin Cowling declared.

Around the world, from the *Dwight D. Flysenhower* aircraft carrier to Japanese sushi bars to pubs in Britain to Mexican cantinas, everyone cheered Dusty's victory!

"For the first time," Brent said, "a crop duster has won the Wings Around The Globe Rally!"

Dusty touched down, ecstatic, the finish-line ribbon still draped over him. El Chu and Rochelle landed neck and neck behind him. Bulldog and Ishani soon followed.

"*Magnifique,* Dusty!" Rochelle said.

"You really kicked his bottom, lad!" Bulldog said, smiling.

Reporters instantly surrounded Dusty, but Dottie and Chug managed to push their way through the crowd. "All right, yeah! Now, *that's* how to pass!" Chug said to Dusty.

"You did it!" Dottie added.

"I couldn't have done it without you," he said.

Dottie smiled and said, "Yeah, I know."

Next Dusty looked at Chug. "Hey, buddy, great tip about Ripslinger leaning to the cameras. Thanks, Chug!"

"Anything for my pal," Chug said, beaming.

Ishani roll up to congratulate Dusty. "Well done!" she said, smiling. "The world has a new champion— and so do I."

"Thanks," Dusty replied. "For everything." He was happy they were friends again.

Then, to Dusty's surprise, Franz appeared with

a group of trucks, planes, tugs, and other working vehicles. "You are an inspiration to all of us who want to do more than just what we were built for," he said.

Meanwhile, Ripslinger had lost control and crashed into a row of portable toilets! Dusty and his friends watched as his humiliated rival was hauled onto the back of a flatbed truck, dripping in oil slop.

A race official took one whiff and said, "*Whew-wee!* Rip*stinker*! Yeah, that's your name. You need to go home and wash up. Twice!"

Suddenly, all eyes turned to the sky as Skipper soared majestically overhead. He gave Dusty a knowing smile and then came in for a landing. The new champion and his coach quickly met up with each other in the crowd.

"Thanks, Skip," Dusty said.

"Don't thank me," replied Skipper. "I learned a lot more from you than you ever learned from me."

It wasn't long before an exuberant Chug invited everyone for free gas. "Fuel's on me, everybody!" he said. Dusty chuckled and looked around warmly as his friends celebrated his victory.

EPILOGUE

On board the *Dwight D. Flysenhower,* every jet saluted as Skipper rolled onto the deck. Dusty was right behind him, with a new paint job for the occasion.

"It's an honor to be here," Skipper said to the crew and officers.

"You ready, wingman?" Dusty asked Skipper.

"Roger that!" Skipper replied.

Bravo rolled up to Dusty. "An honorary Jolly Wrench," he said. "How's that feel, Dusty?"

"Feels great!" Dusty declared.

"Back in the saddle again, eh, Skipper?" Echo asked.

"Well, they didn't have these fancy toys the last time I did this!" Skipper said as he and Dusty moved into the catapults.

"Nothin' to it," Dusty said with a grin. "They hook ya up, you nod to the shooter over there"—he nodded, and the shooter saluted them both—"and hang on!"

"Yeeeeeah-heah!" Skipper yelled as the two friends headed into the wild blue yonder together.